Rhythmical Creations

Flairs and Glairs
Publication House

"Rhythmical Creations"

ISBN No: " 978-93-90799-43-5"
1ˢᵗ Edition
Language – English and Hindi

Flairs and Glairs
Publication House
Regd. Under MSME Act.

Disclaimer

This is a work of fiction and solely represent the thoughts of the corresponding authors of the articles. Our editors have tried their best to edit the content of all the authors and check the plagiarism.

All the write-ups in this book are unique and are only published in this book.

In case any plagiarism or error is found, only the author is responsible alone, and not the publisher or the Compilers.

Cover Designing and Book Formatting
Shubham Shah and Ishani Agarwal

Coauthors

Shubham Shah (Founder Flairs and Glairs)
Ishani Agrawal Co- Founder Flairs and Glairs)
Sakshi Barad (Compiler)

1. Ruchika Morghade
2. Vedang Chatte
3. Rashmi Yadav
4. Amit Pandey
5. Mariyam Jariwala
6. S.Vasha Varthini
7. Kavita Chowdry
8. Tuhin Samantray
9. Sumana Saha
10. Neha Tyagi Ambar
11. Meghna Dutta
12. Visakha Khetan
13. Swikriti Rai
14. Shrawan Pradhan
15. Nikhil Pradhan
16. Mayan Jain
17. Rishi Shrivatsava
18. Sanskriti Singh
19. Neha Singhal
20. Manisha Sharma
21. MOUSUMI SEN
22. Mohammad Nayeem khan
23. Sahina Ghugha
24. Aditi Turkar
25. Kareena Verma
26. Shagufta K Qadri
27. Archishman Satpathy

28. Garvita Gour
29. Aakanshya Mishra
30. Meena Tiwari
31. Mansi Bhatt
32. Shaily Saroj
33. Bandish Panchal
34. Saurabh Tripathi
35. Abhishek Sharma
36. Mohsin Shadab
37. Moni Chaudhary
38. Shubham Rane
39. Govind Joshi
40. Gaurav Dubey
41. Meet Dixit
42. Pramesh Kumar
43. Anjali Samundre
44. Aisha Chhetri
45. Divyanshu Pande
46. Prachi Sharma
47. Priyanka Tiwari
48. Raza Sahil
49. Vijay Thakur
50. Meet Dixit

Shubham Shah

(Founder- Flairs and Glairs)

Shubham Shah, an entrepreneur at "Flairs & Glairs" a brand with dynamics in events organizing and cultural educational pan INDIA, is a 26yrs old guy who recently has entered the digital platform of imprinting emotions. He has initiated with his own open mic platform to help budding poets and aspiring writers under his brand named as "Teekhe Zasbaaat"

He is a commerce graduate from the Bhagalpur City of Bihar. He states Writing has impersonated him since childhood and he has now been writing for over a decade!

Cooking, on the other hand, is his passion! He also mentions, trying out new things just tickles him!

When asked sir, Why SPICY EMOTIONS?

He smiled and added, "agar jasbaat teekhe na ho toh wo jasbaat kahan" Spices are all that blends! So do his words!

As a chef, he presents to you his dish! Hot and freshly served! Taste it! Feel it! Enjoy it! You can also find his writing in the Book "Teekhe Zasbaaat" and 50+ Co-authored anthologies. With his passion to explore opportunities across Platforms, he is working with keen devotion and We wish him all the very best for his future ventures.

He is Featured in the International Magazine DeMode for his upcoming solo novel.

He is Approved by Ne8x for its Lit Fest, and is a Golden Star Awards 2020 Winner.

He is a India Book of Records Holder for his Anthology Satrang, and has the Grandmaster title by Asia Book of Records, for the same.

He has also been featured in Prabhat Khabar, Dainik Jagran, and a lot of other Newspapers in Bihar for his achievements.

He has been a proud co-author to

India Book Of Records (Title- Black)

World Book Of Records (Title -15 Wonders of Poetries)

India Book Of Records (Title - Aaina)

Vajra World Records Holder (Title - Gustakhi Maaf Hai)

High Range of Records Holder (Title - Gustakhi Maaf Hai)

Indian Book of Records

(Title - Road from Worst to Best)

Share your reviews on his

INSTAGRAM

@spicy_emotions
@shubham4shah

Or via email on

shubham2shah@gmail.com

To stay tuned to his work and opportunities follow his business Handles

INSTAGRAM   FACEBOOK   YOUTUBE

@flairsandglairs
@teekhezasbaaat

WEBSITE:

https://flairsandglairs.in/
https://flairsandglairs.com/

Ishani Agarwal

(Co-Founder- Flairs and Glairs)

Ishani Agarwal hails from the City of Joy, Kolkata.
She is the co-founder of her Community "Teekhe Zasbaaat" and Flairs and Glairs Publication.
Been a Compiler for 45+ Anthologies, she is in the process for more. Co-authored in 150+ Anthologies. She is a India Book of Records Holder, a Vajra World Records Holder, a High Range of Records Holder, an OMG Book of Records Holder, a Bravo Record holder, a Forever Star Book of World Records and an Indian Book of Records Holder.
Approved by Ne8x for its Lit Fest 2020, and Literary Icon 2020. Also a Golden Star Awards Winner 2020.
She has also been awarded with India Star Republic Award 2021, a part of She Awards by Awards Arc and Winner of Nari Samman 2021 by Literoma.

She is also selected as Best Achiever of the Year by AwardsArc and Most Challenging Compiler Award by Spectrum Awards.
She got her first solo Published,a solo Compilation consisting of first 750 contents of hers, titled "Hand That Burnt While Healing".

She has been featured by the National Magazine "Taree Zameen Par" with the title 'unstoppable'.
Also featured in the International Magazine DeMode for her upcoming solo novel, she is proud to write on social issues, and is happy with the love she is receiving.
Connect with her on Instagram: @Ishani_agarwal_quotes / @compilations_so_far

Sakshi Barad

She is writer, orator, author and compiler from Nagpur, Maharashtra. She has completed her Postgraduation in Science. She is public speaker and Winner of many elocution and debate competitions, So awarded as Best Orator. She has represented her district in youth and student parliaments. She has also performed in poetry events.

She is published writer. She writes in Hindi, English and Marathi languages. She is passionate and hardworking and very good human being. Her interest and passion in art and literature inspires her to work in this field even if having a science background.

For contact – Instagram - @sakshibarad.5

Mail id – sakshibarad5@gmail.com

खुदको कर बुलंद...

खुदको इतना कर बुलंद
हवा को तू महसूस कर,
लेकिन तुफानो से भी दोस्ती कर,
खुदको इतना कर बुलंद...!

राह में भलेही गिर,
पर फिर उठके दौड़ ..
खुदको इतना कर बुलंद ..!

पानी की हर एक बुंद की कदर कर,
लेकिन समंदर की गहराई कोभी पार कर..
खुदको इतना कर बुलंद...!

धूप में छाँव की आस ना कर,
लेकिन तपते हुए का भी आसरा बन..
खुदको इतना कर बुलंद ...!

असफलता के डर से पिछे मत मुड़,
असफलता से सिखकर फिर से कोशिश कर..
खुदको इतना कर बुलंद...!

खुदको इतना कर बुलंद
कोई तुम्हें रोक ना पाए,
खुदको इतना कर बुलंद
कोई तुम्हें टोक ना पाए,
खुदको इतना कर बुलंद
कोई तुम्हें हरा ना पाए,
खुदको इतना कर बुलंद
आसमान को भी छू जा....!!!

Ruchika Shrikant Morghade

This is Ruchika Shrikant Morghade hailing from city of oranges nagpur, maharashtra.she had completed b.sc in life sciences and pursuing m.sc in rtmnu campus college nagpur.her aim to being a class one officer and her passion in writting and learning new skills.she is a co-author of more than 10+ anthologies and in future so on.

Dear कंधे,

पापा आज आपको बहुत दिनों बाद पत्र लिख रहा हूं।आज आपकी बहुत याद आ रही थीं। मै सोच रहा था कि आपकी कितनी सारी जिम्मेदारियां होगी, जो मै आज उसे महसूस कर रहा हूं। मुझे पहले तो बहुत साधारण सी लगती थीं, अब मुझे उसका एहसास होने लगा है। पहले तो यू आपके कंधों में यूं सो जाता था मैं, अब वहीं कंधों पर कितनी जिम्मेदारियां होंगी उससे वाकिफ हो रहा हूं। आज जब मैं दूसरों के लिए, मै कंधा बनकर खड़ा हूं, तो आपके कंधों का भार कितना होगा इससे वाकिफ हो रहा हूं। यू पहले तो, आपके हाथों में हाथ डालकर और इन नन्हे से कंधों पर बैग लादकर स्कूल जाया करता था। तब नहीं पता था कि, उस हथेली पर कितनी सारी सांसे गुजारा करती थीं। आज समझ आ रहा है कि आप उस वक़्त इतने सख्त क्यू हुआ करते थे। आज पता चला है कि आप मेरे कंधों को धिरे धिरे मजबूत करने की कोशिश करते थे,की जब कोई भी कठिनाईया आए तो उस वक़्त मेरे कंधे डगमगाए नहीं और मै उस चुनौतियां का डटकर सामना करता रहूं। पहले आप मेरे लिए कंधा बनकर खड़े रहते थे, आज मै किसी और के लिए कंधा बनकर खड़ा हूं। जब मैं छोटा था, तो आपको हर बार पुछा करता था कि, आपके आंखों में कभी आंसु क्यू नहीं दिखते। आपने इसका जवाब तो कभी दिया नहीं लेकिन उसका भी जवाब आज मुझे मिल गया। की अगर कंधे ही रोने लगे तो सारा परिवार किस कंधों के सहारे रहेगा। आज आपकी सारी ज़िम्मेदारियों से वाक़िफ हो गया हूं। सब आपकी ही सीख की वज़ह से आज मैं यहां खड़ा हूं और आपकी ही राहों पर चलने की कोशिश कर रहा हूं।

आपने आपका किरदार तो बहुत अच्छे निभाया, अब मेरी पारी है। मै भी अपनी ज़िम्मेदारियां अच्छे से निभाऊ उसके लिए आशिर्वाद दीजिए।

बहुत बहुत शुक्रिया पापा।

Vedang Chatte

Writer .
Orator :- speaker of National Students Parliament 2019 and
Speaker of Vidarbha Students Parliament 2017, 2019.
Anchor.

बेमकसद आसमान में झाकता हु मैं,
पता नही किस चीज़ को तलाशता हु मैं।
इस चाँद के साथ चलती काली घटाओ के समंदर में, शायद किसी
मुसाफिर को ढूंढता हु मैं।
कोई अपना है मेरा जो आसमान मे बैठ कर देखता है ,
या फिर आसमान ही मेरा है जो खैरियत पूछते रहता हु मैं।

Rashmi Yadav

She is Rashmi Yadav. She is from Uttar Pradesh. She is a coming up bud, as she loves to write her emotions through their pen and paper.she is an student by Profession .she believes in "Being yourself whatever the circumstances".

दुनिया में बढ़ते अपराध

दुनिया में बढ़ते अपराधो के पीछे ,किसी मज़बूरी का नाम तो नहीं दे सकते

अपने स्वार्थ के लिए ,दुसरो के घर को उजाड़कर उसे सुकून का आलम तो नहीं कह सकते

इंसान होकर, इंसानियत खोकर ,अपराधों के रास्तो पर चलने वालो को इंसान तो नहीं कह सकते

और बार -बार इंसान को भी तो दोषी नहीं ठहरा सकते ,जब सरकार ही बढ़ावा दे हर क्रूरतियों को समाज में

जो वाकिफ ना थे लोगो और सरकारों की काली करतूतों से वो आज इस दौर को देखकर कहते है क्या ऐसे भी अप्रत्याशीत अपराध, है इस समाज में

जिन्होंने बुराइयों के खिलाफ उठायी आवाज़े उन्हें वीर ना कह कर मुज़रिम नाम देकर कुचल दिए जाते है इस समाज में देश बड़ा है, तो सरकार भी अनेक है, पर जब काम ना हो

बक्सी और पैसा खाने के हो आदि तो बहाने भी हज़ारो होते है

पर क्या करे, यही सच्चाई है इस समाज की आज हर अपराध समायोजित है ,इस समाज में|

Human A Package Of Attributes

Be the world of your Parents
Be the hearts of your little one's
Be the ego of your struggled and succeed life
Be the owner of your own world
Be the Personality of good behaviour and attire
Be the satisfaction for what you have
Be the motive of every good work and talk
Be the mystery of beginning a useful work.

Amit Pandey

Amit Pandey is an Advocate at Patna High Court, a poet and a writer who is coming up with this amazing anthology "Rythmical Creations"
Instagram @mera_karwa Personal id @pande_yamit01
Email immyrj.kumar@gmail.com

मेरी एक जिंदगी

मेरी जिंदगी कि बस इतनी सी कहानी है,
कभी शुरु हुई थी तुमसे और तुमपे ही एक दिन खतम हो जानी है।

बंदिश

आ ज़रा साथ बैठ पल भर के लिए की इस दिल में कोई रंजिश नहीं
तेरे लिए,
चले जाना शौख से जब तेरा जी करे की ये इश्क है यहा कोई बंदिश
नहीं तेरे लिए।

Mariyam Jariwala

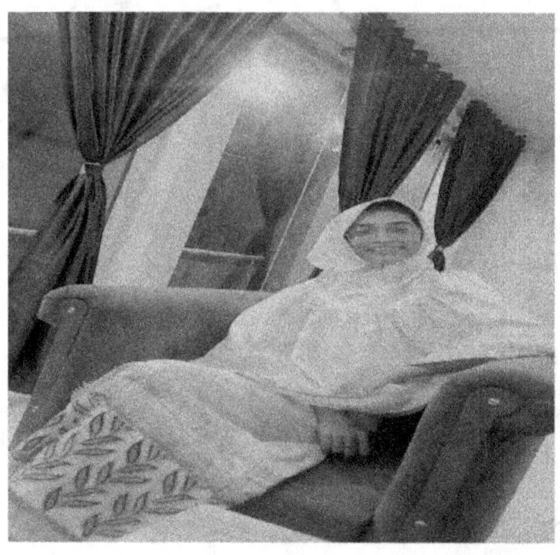

Mariyam is a young girl with loads of sparkle in her eyes.She started potrating her words into poetry 3 years ago.she observe things around her and than potrait those things into mesmerizing poems.

Season OF LIFE

Be with me in the every season of life
In winters,
Be the warmness to my soul, And the blanket to my secretes.

In summers,
Be the calmness to my soul, And my guide In the tour of life.

Lastly,
In monsoons
Be the shelter to my wounds, And the handler to my moods.

The way season changes……
In the same manner
Seasons in our life also keeps on changing
So,be with me and hold on to me in the every season of life

The Rose Is Dead

The rose is dead
But it still contains the fragrance of memories we made
The color of rose has changed
And in the same manner our life has changed after we
separated
The rose has no smeel left it in
Slowly slowly the petals are falling off
But,The words
Feelings and emotions
We shared
Our not falling of from my heart
It's being years
The rose is dead

S. Vasha Varthini

Creative person with optimistic vibes. Working as assistant professor in department of English. Love to learn new things always. Happy person with sheer enthusiasm. Explore the world through writing. Provoke of thought penned through writing

Crazy Wish

Shout with sound of falls
Dance in the highway
Get locked in favourite mall
Become invisible
Wake up with flower around
Stay two place at a time
Float in the air
Adventure thrilling experiance
Travel with unknown to unknown
Night spent with middle of waters

Lost in island
Meet under ocean
Feel the fairy world
Lie on beach and count stars for hours
Craziness fills in each wish
Its in you. . Bring out. .
Live crazy filled. .
Spice to normality. .

Kavita Chowdry

Her name is Kavita Chowdry and she is persuing Journalism and right now she is working as a freelance content writer. She has worked as co- author in many books and she looking forward to work more in this field.

Friendship

From sitting alone to munching Lays
Resting on your shoulder when I'm down
Irritating you with my continuous nonsense chatter
Eagerly waiting for you in the college canteen
Nubble on your head with a pile of complaints and gossips
Dedicating songs to you on radio
Sending each other love through small notes and flowers
Helping each other in every bump of life
Investing in each other's dreams
Praying for each other's health and so on, from minor to
major things I got your friendship. I got you, I got a friend.

Tuhin Samantray

Tuhin was born and raised in the temple city of Bhubaneshwar in the states of Odisha, India. Though he has suddenly developed a keen urge to express his feelings in paper and ink, he is still more into numbers and mathematics. When asked to choose between one, he says, " I inhale the magic of poetry in numbers. If I stop counting the star dust, this magic will fade. " He resists being called a poet. He says," Poetry is and has always been a way of expressing myself."

Eternal Love

I dropped by a garden of Roses
And ambled through the thorns in rain.
Here and there I searched a lot
Knowing it was all in vain
Beauty that my sight can't hold
Made my heart full of love and pain
Then pink, the sky, had now turned black
Emptied heart - once stolen
Whispers unspoken words of love and joy.
Memories keep flashing, promises left broken Faded aura of the rosy winds
Makes my heart full of love and pain.

Dreamgirl

Play the strings
With her magic fingers
She sat singing
An endless song
Slow blows the autmn wind
Beauty blooms her wonder smile
Drops and drapes her silver hair
Time has paused its endless flow
Far she goes with the setting sun
Swift her hands, move then and now
And fades my dream
In her endless eyes

Sumana Saha

A software engineer turned MBA-HR professional, she takes special interest in dancing, writing & social work. She has written content for several startups, magazines, online pages, writing communities & blogs including her own blog Masqueraded Insurgence, and also published poems & stories with several publication houses.

The Coveted Spring

The coveted spring, Sprang up within,
Hoodlums of the nature..
Pathetic creature...
Their lecherous peep, Still way too deep...lies
Failed courtship with their stomach...
Weeks, since the last crumb.. Of bread that slithered in ..
Lullabying hunger in broken slumber
Yet still awed by that cruel fruit..
That hangs above...And shows him his place..
Mocking his debility….The hoodlums of nature..
Pathetic creature..The castaway was here...
And they say spring feeds all...?

Tricolor

Days were colorless when both of us left home,
Everyday our country land used to bathe in a pool of gory.
You went abroad to study while I stayed back,
Only to witness people staring at the twilight skies
Waiting for a ray of hope amid the blend of light and dark.
Finally it all ended.
And on this day you return.
I can see you but you can't see me.
I can see your nine year old waving the tricolor;
And you, with teary eyes,
 looking at my uniform and medals around.
Slowly you walk up to my photo on the wall with a garland,
With a shivering voice,
you utter "Happy Independence Day, Major."

Neha Tyagi Ambar

She is a young, talented writer and already worked on several books. She is also a philanthropist and an animal lover. She wishes to make a change and aware people through her writing skills. Her dream is to open a rescue home for the voiceless and deprived. She awaits your feedback and don't forget to check out her Instagram handle : @aambar_1995

जज़्बात

दो बूंद जब बंज़र ज़मी को सेहलाया करती है,
नराज़्गी मुद्दतो की जब खत्म हो जाया करती है,
जब किसी प्यासे को दो घुंट पानी नसीब हुआ करता है,
जेसे किसी मा से उसका बिछडा बच्चा करीब हुआ करता है ।
रुबरुह हो जाता है खुदा
 जब सुखे पत्ते हरे हुआ करते है,
हमे मंदिरो-मज़ारो से क्या लेना,
हम तो इबादत जज़्बात की करते हैं ।
तपती धूप में जब नन्ही सी छाव दिखा करती है,
बेरुखी होटो से जब भाप बना करती है,
थंड मे सेक जब रुह तक पहुचा करता है,
जैसे किसी भुखे जानवर का पेट भरा करता है,

रुबरुह हो जाता है खुदा,
जब मरहम ज़ख्म पर लगने से दिल भरा करते है
हमे मंदिरो-मज़ारो से क्या लेना,
हम तो इबादत जज़्बात की करते हैं ।
जब फिज़ाओ में रंग बिखरा करता है,
किसी बीज का जब फुटाव हुआ करता है,
जब हवाओ मे नर्मी हुआ करती है,
जैसे मोहोब्बत का आगाज़ हुआ करता है
रुबरुह हो जाता है खुदा,
जब हम कुद्रत का एह्तराम करते है,
हमे मंदिरो-मज़ारो से क्या लेना,
हम तो इबादत जज़्बात की करते हैं ।

Meghna Dutta

Myself Meghna Dutta, writing is my passion. It was started just 2years before , i discovered this talent in me. Right now doing masters in biotechnology and apart from that i am the co - author of 9books and two of them created world record. I am sure these numbers will increase in the coming future.

कुछ बातें ऐसे भी

खामोशियों की कोई आवाज नहीं होती,
आंसुओं की कोई कदर नहीं होती।
गलती की कोई माफी नहीं होती,
पर हर गलती की सजा मौत नहीं होती।
प्यार हमेशा दो तरफा नहीं होता,
इश्क हमेशा एक तरफा नहीं होता।
हर इश्क मुकम्मल नहीं होता,
पर हर कहानी की सेड एंडिंग नहीं होती।

मुमकिन है प्यार में लोग जान दे दे,
मुमकिन तो यह भी है कि प्यार किसी की जान ले ले,
मुमकिन यह भी है कि प्यार की कोई हद ना हो,
प्यार एक पल का तो नहीं,
प्यार कुछ पल का भी नहीं होता,
प्यार तो पल पल का मेहमान है,
पर हर प्यार की किस्मत में कमाल नहीं होता।

Visakha Khetan

A growing writer, who writes to express the emotions within and let people learn from her lessons. A singer by heart with the soul of a writer. Someone who wants to inspire people with her experiences.

Ig handle: visakhakhetan_2202
Quote Id: the_nostalgic_writer
Mail id: visakhakhetan2122@gmail.com

Tere sath sab sahi lage ,
Ek ummr bhi tere sath kam lage ,
Tu aankhe padh leti h meri har baar ,
Tu hi h mere jiwan ka saar .
Bas kuch choti baatain h jo kehni h tujhse ,
Tu kabhi dur na jaana mujhse ,
Dil se khush raha kar tu ,Tujhse judi h meri rooh .
Tujhe bata nhi paya ki kitna pyaar h mere dil mai tere liye ,
Par has k tere ko gham bhi maine le liye ,
Tu paas nhi h mere ab ,Par tu jinda h mujh mai ye kehte h sab.
Tu h mujhe kahi na kahi ,Na jaane ye lakire kya kar rahi ,
Sab ko lagta h tu dur jaa raha h unse...Tu nhi meri jeene ki wajah cheen raha h rab mujhse.

Swikriti Rai

 Swikriti Rai from Darjeeling. She is doing college now. Started writing poetry as hobby but now it have became the part of her life..
Writing gives her immense peace ..it's like Bestfriend who is with her both in happiness and grief..

The Poetry Of The Poet

When sunset settles down
Here comes the rumor of his own
From the soul to the heart
From the heart to the hand
And sits camly beside specs
Glittering pearl from the eye
To open up the agony.
Every phrase is evoking him,
She was his authentic one,but Now only reminiscence could
call Like an old nostalgia!
Now the darling is the paper
Where he ink
The poetry is the poet Deeply craving himself.
Our half hearts
Yet it is the midest summer
We were gazed in frozen winter,
We will intacted in harsh autumn,
We can shade our leaves in the form of heart!
But the important is soul like trunk in autumn
Who stand straight And wait the leaves to crul green,
When we had half beating hearts
We shared our pieces with each other
And waited the spring to be greenish
Today we have our full heart Healed and justified
Neither every pieces is mine Nor every pieces is yours;We
mixed it, So,my every beat consist you
And your every beat consist me..

Shrawankumar Pradhan

Thinker and Achiever.I am Shrawankumar Pradhan from darjeeling hills! I am doing my graduation. Writing is like breathing for me..I write poems and gazals in nepali language too.. writing was hobby for me but now it's my passion..

She's In Love.

Every morning from the beats of own ,
she gets massage a great.
And comes the noon,
With the bright light,
Where future knocks
The door of her.
With a peaceful dawn,
Rests her body,
In the room of tight hug,
In the arms of beloved,
Falls a little more,
Down in Love, With him everyday. After a busy day
Lastly, her heart Massages.
She's in love again.

Nikhil Pradhan

I am Nikhil pradhan from Darjeeling tukdha tea estate pursuing my degree in geography..poetry,it's not my profession but it's the collection of my feelings and emotions which I love to express in words and I wanna go deep down with it..

A New Day

Here is a new day New morning with bright sunshine.
And a "new me"
Painting my life with colourful crayons...
Those crayons that were left broken...
A step of building oneself...
An assurance of caring self...
A new journey,to build oneself brawny from innerself..
Filling all those scars with blessings..
And after a long rain,
Waiting for a bright and pellucid sky..
Learning lessons, forgiving oneself..
And at the end of the year,
Giving all those painful memories a happy good bye..

Oh Moon!!

Oh moon!
You are so astonishing.
No beauty can be compare with you .
You are an inspiration.
The inspiration for those,
who are scared of darkness.
You inspire them ,
with your bright light .
The light that shines bright,
even in the darkness.
You are hope.You are strength.
You are believe that ,Even in lonliness.
One can perfectly shine.

Mayank Jain

"Whisper of pains through my veins
World of lies according to my pen."
MBA graduate
Entrepreneur
Survivor.

All my life I never felt ashamed, Because I had never been flamed,
Not burn by fire,
But by someone's desire,
I feared to look into a piece of glass,
The one who wouldn't fear had now been drowned in the tallgrass,
The thought of how I would look gave me distress,
But the one who did this was not even in stress,
 I decided to take the fight alone to be throned,
 But there were more like me who were dethroned,
To put an end to this kind of desire,
 We now pledge to fight with undying fire,
We have lost our face by burning,
But we won't stop until the culprits would be shivering.
Warrior, not 'a victim'.
We struggle the most when we fall,
We look around at the night sky,
It seems people are stars but the one you love is moon,
The star may twinkle and yes the moon may dissapear for a while,
And we might feel that we are captivated by those stars when the moon's not there,
But we all know what the love of our life "The Moon" means to us,
And it always comes back to brighten our life with their glow.

Rishi Srivastava

He is Rishi Srivastav born and raised in Lucknow. Presently pursuing B. Com. His ethic is" never neglect an opportunity for improvement "
He likes reading books mostly related to shayari and Gazal..
He enjoys writing about various human emotions

जुर्म की सजा मिली मुझे
चोरी की सजा मिली मुझे
या खुदा ।।
इश्क़ किया मैंने
सजा दे ना मुझे

मोहब्बत का मंजर बहोतो का देखा
कहा था अपनो ने मोहब्बत एक खंजर हैं
बहुत दर्द देगी तुझे

मलहम की तलाश में मोहब्बत फिर मिलेगी
दोस्त........
मीठा जहर हैं
खत्म कर देगी तुझे ।।

Sanskriti Singh

She believes in Valuing reality than fantasy, and give Priority to harsh truths than sweet lies. She is sanskriti and she is of 13 years, young eyes with a lot of dreams. She is from a small city 'Bokaro' and she want that Bokaro will be known by her name.. she love to do new innovating activities but her personal favourite is helping others. And everyone suggested her to go ahead for a simple life but she believes humans are the most superior creature on earth and if God had given us a chance to be that then we should also make it special.

Love Yourself

Why people search others to understand there feelings,
When you have to stand alone in the process of healing.
You have to solve your own problem.
Because people have time to judge you but they don't have
patience to hold your hands when you are in trouble..

Neha Singhal

One part of her wants to give up while the other keeps going. Neha Singhal is an introvert until someone initiates, who believes that can of worms is not variants in the vicinity rather you yourself. She is a writer who kisses him poetically everyday and her sould bleeds through her pen.
Connect with Neha via-Ig-@till_grey

Iss Chahat Me Mar Jayenge

Kisi ko na hongi aisi chahatein,Pal pal badhti ye
mohabattein,
Karta hai ye dil teri hi baatein,Dubara kaise ho vo haseen
mulakaatein.
Hasta hai ye dil bass tujhe hi sochkar, Unn paalo ko iss seene
me lapet kar,
Tu bhi kabhi unhe yaad kar, Mujhe usi tarah pyaar kar.
Kabhi na socha tha tu milega,
Or iss seene me yun thamega,
Mujhe beech raah me chod jaega,
Fir wapas kabhi na aaega, Or aakhir me keh jaega,
Main tera na ho paunga. Fir vo ishq adhoora reh gaya, Or
mujhe ye keh gaya,
Tu bhul jaa uss pal ko, Par ye dil mukar gaya,
Kyunki hokar ye tera reh gaya.
Shayad tujhe kabhi na paa saku,
Par itna tujhe pyaar karu,
Ke tera naam lekar hi aakhri sans lu,
Or aakhir me bhi ye bol du,
Tum hi the, tum hi ho or tum hi
rahoge.
Chah kar bhi na tujhe bhula paenge,
Yuhi isqh me pagal ho jaenge,
Ek din tumhe apna banaenge,
Isi khyal me khush ho jaenge,
Or fir ek baar teri mohabbat me mar jaenge,
Haste haste sab seh jaenge,
Tere pyaar ko taras jaenge,
Par tujhe kabhi na bhula paenge,
Iss chahat me mar jaenge.

Manisha Sharma

Manisha Sharma from Pali Rajasthan is an Assistant Professor in Commerce and Management Studies by Profession and a Writer by Passion. She is pursuing her Phd in Accounting. She is co-author of various anthologies. She believes that "Either write something worth reading or do something worth writing." You never have to change anything you got up in the middle of the night to write. Her Instagram handles are @manisha_sharma1729 and @sachhi_kalam1709. You can contact her on manishasharma1729@yahoo.com

महत्त्वपूर्ण क्या है??

दीपक मिट्टी का है या सोने का,
यह महत्त्वपूर्ण नहीं है।
बल्कि वो अंधेरे में,
प्रकाश कितना देता है,
यह महत्त्वपूर्ण है।
उसी तरह मित्र गरीब है या अमीर,
यह महत्त्वपूर्ण नहीं है।
बल्कि वो आपकी मुसीबत में आपका कितना साथ देता है,
यह महत्त्वपूर्ण हैं।
आसान तो कुछ भी नहीं है,
इस संसार में,
एक सांस लेने के लिए भी,
पहली सांस छोड़नी पड़ती हैं।

" वो परिन्दा उड गया "

वो परिन्दा उड गया है,
जिसका तू रखवाला था।
पिंजरे से नहीं था उसका नाता,
उसे तो खुला आसमान प्यारा था।।
जितना चाहता है अब वो,
उतने पंख फैलाएगा |
नई उड़ान भरकर वो
आसमान से टकराएगा ||
सुबह कहीं तो ,
शाम कहीं और कर जाएगा
तिनका तिनका जोड़ कर परिंदा,
अपना नया आशियाना बनाएगा ||
होंगे इरादे मजबूत तो,
तूफानों से टकरा जाएगा ||

Mousumi Sen

A Student Of High School, Born And Currently Residing In The Steel City, Jamshedpur. Now Trying Her Capabilities To Create Some Good Writeups From Her Self Made Imagination. She Also Has A Wish To Publish Er Own Book. She Wries To Experss Herself Through The Words Which Hides Her Feelings And Thoughts Inside Them.

Sudden Pull

So She Knew It Was The Time To Bid Him A Farwell,
But He Wont Leave Her Easily Was Secretly Planned And
Then Loudly Yelled.
As She Turned Around And Made Her Way To Leave,
Her Grabbed And Pulled Her Tightly By Her Waist,
There Was A Certain Astonishment Shown On Her Face But
She Didnt Move,
He Was Being Desperate And Restless To Feel Her Was
Clealry Being Proved.
He Pushed Her On His Chest And Held Her Hands Tight,
She Was Numb And Speechless By The Dazzling Spark In His
Eyes.
He Pulled Her Neck Firmlly And Felt The Thrombing Beats
Of Heart,
And That's When She Melted And Felt How The Horizons
Were Falling Apart.
After Feeling Every Inch Of Her Lips And Face, He Lastly
Ended By Hugging Her Tight.
She Was Blushing And Gazed At Him Silently While Her
Face Was Shinning All Bright.

Mohammad Nayeem khan

He is Mohammad Nayeem khan. He lives in Kashmir Srinagar batamaloo. Qualification master of R.I.M in Assam. Having a busy schedule has not sidelined his love for words. He writes enchanting shayris which have always charmed the listeners. Here, it's a chance for you all also to enjoy it. He loves to pen down his spontaneous thoughts with a tinge of magic in them.You can connect with him through these...Insta ID-K_nayeem_

Kahtai Thai DADU kissi giear ko Apni kamzoori nai bolna,
Manai apna samaj k uss sai aapni kamzoori boldi,
Uss nai uss kamzoori ko najayizz faidaii Uthai k muj j sallou
k baid mairai DADU ki yaad Dilla dii.

Yaadai

Wo sardi ka mohsaam doupair ka waqt,jahnay q maira mood
Thai shaqait.
Wo sumsan si galiya wo gali you Mai Touf,jahnay q mairai
Dil Mai Thai khouf.
*Lamba Thai raistai dimai Thai kadaam,jahnay q maira Chara
Pai Thai gaam.
*Wo moosam ka badail nai barish ka gernai,jahnay q muj Mai
kissi ki thi khuwaish.
*Wo patou ka geernai,bagho Mai Thai daier ,jahnay q woh
Pochti harkissi sai mairai khair.
*Wo bagh Mai Thai doo phoolo ka mail,jahnay q ussnai mairai
sth khaila khel.
Wo rouh Mai ahwaaz ahwaaz Mai rouh ,jahnay q muj j milli
hameshn tou.Wo itnai sai saafar bht si baitai,jahnay muj j q
milli akhir lattai. Ussai muj j deak k q hotii thii hairani,jahnay
q yai Kahani kahtaam howi yahiii.....

Sahina Ghugha

Sahina Ghugha is 20 year old b.com student at Saurashtra university Rajkot. She is from Jamnagar city of Gujarat. She is state level winner in poetry competition 2017. She is Co-author of 15+ anthologies. She is an amazing writer and poet and she wants do something for society through her pen.
Insta ID:- Itz_Sahina_write

तुम्हारी बातों में दिल आ गया था
तुम्हारा चेहरा मुझको भा गया था

बस नज़र भर तुमको देखकर ही
दिल मेरा तुम्हें साजन बना गया था

बस रहे थे सांसों में तुम धीरे धीरे
तुम्हारा सुरूर घटा सा छा गया था

मैं नही जानती थी तेरी चालाकियां
तेरा झूठा वादा मुझे फंसा गया था

शौक था मुझे लिखने का बहुत
तेरा धोखा लिखा और गा दिया था

Aditi Turkar

She is Aditi Turkar Doughter of Dileep&Rajeshwari Turkar
Student of 'computer science'
"आता कुछ नहीं,
लेकिन करना सब कुछ चाहती हूं ।
आज कुछ सीखकर, कुछ समझकर,
अपने कल को संवारना चाहती हूं ।"

"अब जरूरी सा हो गया"

अब जरूरी सा हो गया है,कदम बढ़ाना....
आराम के दलदल से पांव निकालने की,
जरा सी मशक्कत तू कर जाना....
सोचते तो सब हैं,लेकिन तू एक सबक दे जाना....
"कल" तो सारे जग को भाया है,
मान मेरी बात,तुझे तो आज को है अपनाना....
बस याद रखना जानी,
सूरज की चमक में इन्सान ने अपने,
"चंदा मामा" को भी ना पहचाना....
अरे! तू भी तो सितारा है,एक दिन चमकेगा,
क्योंकि सहीं वक्त हर एक का है आना...
अब जरुरी सा हो गया है,कदम बढ़ाना ।

" खुशियां और मै"

क्यों हर वक्त,
खुशियां मुझ तक आते-आते रुक जाती हैं,
क्यों मेरी चाहतों को,
मेरी तकदीर पूरा नहीं कर पाती है,
भूलना चाहूं,हुआ था जो कल को,
तो क्यों,
याद करने के लिए एक नई बात आ जाती है,
ए खुदा.... बता तू आज मुझे,
आखिर क्यों तेरी रहमत भी मुझे आजमाती है,
और क्यों हर वक्त,
खुशियां मुझ तक आते-आते रुक जाती हैं.....

Kareena verma

She is kareena verma The Daughter of Mr.Kehru verma & Mrs.Rajeshwari verma . She is a computer science student and currently pursuing the bachelor of application And she is very passionate in writing and co- author of many anthologies and as well as many international Anthologies too. In this world only her pen & diary is the best friend to penned her pain in the blank pages of life Diary .And same as her name Kareena delineate alike her name , sanguine with her soul, pure with her heart , innocent with her straightforward thoughtful perceptions!For her Rectitude within her is everything & nothing is above than Viracity with our nation , she wants only to flame alike terracotta Diya, for one day she'll spread the happiness of lights as the most bright star in the sky of someone home and just wanna to spread love of humanity every where !!

When You Trust Yourself,

When you trust yourself,
Disheartenment within you with full of gappy,
Looking alike you're not Happy!
Discover yourself more to know your endurable,
To made within you believable!
I knew your ambiance in you,
That's how much passionate potential in you !
Don't take-apart yourself because of someone,
Let them woof those someone!
Lord Krishna is here with law of karma,
So you do great deeds within your pure karma!
Indeed!

Every Writer Was A Once

Every writer was a once
Faced the Despondency in past,
But the bitterness at the last,
Made you better from your past,
To know more about yourself,
Let the people judge you for your forte!
There's a lot who don't let you live !
But they've not known the virtuosity in you !

Shagufta K Qadri

Shagufta K Qadri is a poet, a reviewer, a thinker, an educator, mentor, trainer, bibliophile and a blogger. She has done MA in English Literature. She is a regular contributor to various National and International Anthologies. A regular contributor on FB online poetry groups.

"Wo Khamosh Cheekhein"

Ajnabee shahar ne ye kesa dard diya
Bas ek durghatna ne mera sab kuch chhin liya
Behti khushiya thi us shahar me mere sang
Ek gehra dard mujhe tohfe me de diya
Rangeen thi zindagani meri bhi kabhi
Lab muskurate the surkh pankhudi ki tarah
Mauje behti thi jaha se gujar jati thi kabhi
Sab kehte the tujhse hi ronak-e-mehfil hoti he
Us din ka wo akalam bhi kya tha
Cheekhon me mujhe kisi apne ne utha kar utara
Bas afra tafri me mere zinda hone ki hi khabar thi
Hosh to unke bhi fakhta the jinki mein jaan thi
Sabki nazre ghadi pe tiki thi
Doctor kya kehti he bas iska intezar tha
Nam aankhein chupke se dekh jati thi
Koi andar ro raha tha to koi behaal khada tha
Laga jese samandar khushiyan kha gaya ho
Nafrat ke sailab sa koi mera asteetav nigal gaya ho
Jo mere apne mere sath the, meri himmat maan gaye Us
accident ka asar ab bhi baki he
Zindagi ke kuch pal hansate he to kuch rulate he
Wo pal esa tha na cheekh saki na ro saki
Un khamosh cheekon ki gunj me bas tarapti rahi
Jab doctor ne chhutti ke waqt kaha kabhi mamta na bikher
sakogi
Besudh si, behaal si, khud ka bhojh uthati chali
Zinda laash si bas pal pal aage badhti chali
Tarap jati he rooh aksar uski khwahish me Jise mein kabhi paa
na saki……….!!

Archishman Satpathy

Archishman Satpathy, often called the Enthusiast Writer is a young dynamic writer from Deogarh, Odisha. He is presently pursuing B.Tech from IIIT Bhubaneswar. He started writing Quotes and Short Poetries from a young age of 16 and had now made it as his passion. He has contributed as co-author in more than 180 anthologies. He is the author of the book "LAKEEREIN ZINDAGI KE".

I Am No More Yours

Today you are not mine anymore
That deepest is that endeavour???
You tried to be controlled right?
Again the same thinking in sight
I must have stopped you from that
That gave you the freedom so apart
We planned for some verses of us
And now left with nothingness
Just the pillars we are followed had broke
The pieces apart are still unable to stroke
I just want that script to be for us
In the golden history of shrine Yes today the night will be harder But tomorrow again the sun will shine

Today Writing Became My Love

Writing became my love,
 when The adolescent kicked me out And the teenage started
ignoring
Letting the failures to conquer
I was unable to live a life with a life
Leading a fortunate edge of greatness
The slider was rolling in a short knife
Shuttling with the conscience
I started focussing on work Just because the form now back
Luck is jumping high like a shark
Then the shot cracked and tore
The day and the happiness apart
When I realised the importance
What Writing gave before depart

Garvita Gour

A budding lawyer, who is very passionate about writing and wakes up with intent to bring smile, hope, positivity and happy vibes in the lives of people.

There's hope in the dark,
and energy in spark.
So Look around and you'll find THE REASON
As now It's time to break the self-made prison.

Don't assume that 'TRYING' will make things easy for you..
But it'll definitely take you closer to the destination that has
been long overdue..

Akankshya Mishra

The escapist
Lost in words

Woman

Tea in hand ,stealing time from my loads
On my terrace mapping the roads.
Born and bought with love and care
Now I stand with a faded flare.
Duties multiplied roles from daughter to mother
But my aspirations were no one's bother..
Beauty of a rose pleasant to eyes
No credit to the thorn that protect them from cries.
So stays a woman standing strong
Enjoying her life serving all.
Penning my thought on this sacrificing sea
Cause to burn and light others
Is not everyone's cup of tea..

Smile

Nothing in this era can stand a chance
A beautiful smile is a healer in glance
Smile to the person you met in ages
May it be strangers, workers or sages.
Gift to the florist ,the rose he sells
Warmth he feels his eyes will tell
Sit aside your family for a little while
The smile on their face shall glam up your style.
Be kind to all but stay special to you
Smile to yourself assume hard time flew
With a morning light you get a hope ray
Stand, rejoice and make it your day.

Meena(Prity)Tiwari

A girl of 16, born and raised in Darjeeling. Someone who dreams to paint the world with the colours she has in her heart . Someone who dreams and finds refuge in pondering her thoughts on paper.

My Love

Keep me in your loving arms,
I will feel warm.
Keep me deep inside your heart,
I will feel safe.
Keep me in your thoughts, I will feel special.
Even if anyone else knocks at the door of my heart,
Promising the entire world,
I know, even a plethora of them won't match the feeling I get
when I'm with you.
You, my love, transcend time and space .
You are my greatest strength and my weakness too.
You are my utopia, where my world begins and ends, You
are My Love.

Manasi Bhatt

Manasi Bhatt - 'The brown eyed girl' is an aspiring Architect, Artist and an instagram poet. She belongs to the Gujarati family background and she has never ending interests in hindi shayries and Ghazals. At the age of 23, she became the founder and writer of 'Inking Emotions'. She has also penned down a few microtales. She dreams of becoming successful Architect and Writer one day!

प्रेम की परिभाषा

धुंआधार बरसती बरसात में
कच्ची छत से टपकती जल बूंदो से उठती ध्वनि
मेरे गम के अश्को की सिसकीयों में विलीन हो गई
उसके आलिंगन में लेते ही
कडकती बिजली के खौफ में
उंगलियों ने जकड़ा उसके तपते बदन को दबाव से
शर्म से गालों पर लाली सी चड गई
दोनों के नजरे चूराते ही
खूली छत के बंध कमरे में
खिड़की से जुड़ी दरारों से निकली सर्द हवाएं
घनी जुल्फों के वक्रो मे गुम सी गई
जब साँसो की गर्मी छायी दो अधरों के मिलते ही

याराना सा लगता है

तुम से मिले हुए कई साल हो गए मगर
आज भी मिलता हूं तो याराना सा लगता है
होठों की लाली आज भी वही है मगर
आँख का काजल दिल को नजराना सा लगता है
गालों को चूमते झुमके, ललाट की लाल बिंदी वही है मगर आँख का
काजल दिल को नजराना सा लगता है
म्रृत सा देह जुडा है आत्मा से मगर
तुझे देख दिल में धडकन का अंकुराना सा लगता है
तुम से मिले हुए कई साल हो गए मगर
आज भी मिलता हूं तो याराना सा लगता है

Saurabh Tripathi

This is Saurabh Tripathi born in Chitrakoot UP. A person who had just finished his Post graduation. But all of the above and more than anything first i am a Writer with Poetic accent.For reading more of me or you can say my writings so go to my instragram page @theworldforwrite . You can also contact me on my your quote id - saurabh_tripathiinstragram - @theworldforwrite. Mail id –
theworldforwrite@gmail.comTwitter - @WorldForWrite

जीवन में छुपी जीवन की परिभाषा,
जैसे नदियों सी बहती है जीने की आशा।
सपनों की लहरों में बहता ही जाता,
कि मंज़िल से पहले ना रुकता समाता।
पंछी सा डालो में भी गुनगुनाता,
जीवन की मूरत को गढ़ता बनाता।
इस उपवन में सौरभ सा मिलता ही जाता,
फिर झरनों में ख्वाबों के दीपक जलता।
इन गीतों को लिखता मै तुमको सुनाता,
जीवन में छुपी जीवन की परिभाषा।
राहों में चलता या राहें बनाता,
खुशियों को भरकर गमों को मिटाता।
चलता या रुकता या बढ़ता ही जाता,
मंज़िल में जाकर भी मंज़िल बनाता।
 बातों ही बातों में तुमको बताता,
जीवन में छुपी जीवन की परिभाषा.....

Shaily Saroj

Her name is Shaily Saroj from Sangam nagri Prayagraj...
She is the college student of Allahabad University...
Her hobbies are poetry writing singing and reading novels...

रिश्ता कागज और कलम का

खाकर इतने धोखे अब दिल को,
कोई रिश्ता ना भाता है,
अब ना प्यार मोहब्बत करने को जी चाहता है,
उस दिन बस इन्हीं ख्यालों में डूबी थी,
और लेकर कलम कर रही थी कागज पर अपने जज्बात बया,
तब महसूस हुआ कि एक रिश्ता भी है कागज और कलम का,
जो है सबसे जुदा सबसे अलग,
एक दूजे के बिना अधूरे से लगते हैं,
सहकर दोनों तकलीफें लिखते हैं नए जज्बात।
एक दिन रुठ कर बैठ गया कागज, कहता है ना दूंगा तेरा साथ,
तुझे तो ना होती है कोई तकलीफ,
कलम हंसकर बोली ना दूंगी तुझको जख्म,
तो तू निखरेगा कैसे,
फेंक देंगे लोग तुझे जब ना तू देगा उनका साथ,
होती हैं मुझे भी तकलीफ अपनी मोहब्बत को यूं हर पल जख्मी करना,
पर कर देंगे जुदा लोग हमे, जब ना करुगी तुझ पर वार,
तब कागज ने बड़े प्यार से बोला,
चल कलम लिखे है हम अपनी मोहब्बत - ए - दास्तां ।।।।

Bandish Panchal

बंदिश पंचाल अहमदाबाद से इलेक्ट्रिक इंजीनियरिंग मैं पढाई कर रहे हैं। पढाई के साथ साथ लिखना, किताबे पढ़ना, क्रिकेट खेलना ,ये सब सोख रखते हैं। उनको दोस्तों एवम् प्रेम के बारे में ज्यादा लिखना पसंद करते हैं। । बंदिश गुजराती ,हिंदी , इंग्लिश मैं लिखना पसंद है। उन्होंने कही सारी anthology book मैं अपनी बातें लिखी हुई है।
Instagram page: marri_vaattoo

परिवार का महत्व...

जो परिवार मैं होती हैं एकता हंमेशा,
वो घर में रहती हैं खुशिया हंमेशा।
जो परिवार में होता हैं संप हंमेशा,
वो घर मैं रहती हैं लक्ष्मी हंमेशा।
जो परिवार मैं होता हैं मिलन हंमेशा,
वो घर मैं बनी रहती हैं पवित्रता हंमेशा।

तु ही नजर आती है....

रात हो या दिन,
तु ही नजर आती है।
दूर हो या नजदीक,
तु ही नजर आती है।
खुश हो या नाराज,
तु ही नजर आती है।

Abhishek Sharma

Abhishek has always been fond of words, patterns and Nature from earliest of age. He soon developed habit of writing everything down and fell in love with poetry and has been writing ever since .
Instagram: Collimated_words

Lost And Found

At the age of five i lost my dad,
I thought i lost everything i had,
Maturity ceased the pain
And slowly i started to smile again.
I lost my first competition i took part,
And i lost many expectations.
I lost my best friend, when he was young,
then I lost myself in the world of drugs ,
I was so lost, i lost the meaning of life and love
I was lost in lust, and virtual reality,
I lost my family,my friends and society,

Few years later, i found myself soaked in blood
Months later i was trying to find the true meaning of life,
Exactly the day , i found her
I found all my answers, Love is the reason ,
i have lost and found my soul.

Mohsin Shadab

Passion:- Poetry Writing
Profession:- Mechanical Engineer
Awarded By Mrs. Kiran Bedi For scoring Higher Rank In
Engineering Examination.
City:- Pulgaon, District Wardha, Maharashtra India

ज़ुल्म अपनी अना पे न ढाए गए
नाज़ तेरे न हम से उठाए गए

थोड़ी ताख़ीर क्या लौटने में हुई
कितने इलज़ाम हम पे लगाए गए

हम को पहले बनाया गया हम नशीं
जामे फुर्क़त हमें फिर पिलाए गए

हो फ़लक पार शायद मयस्सर सुकूँ
हम ज़मीं पे तो हर जा सताए गए

शहर भर से तो उठनी ही थीं उंगलियां
फिर भला किस लिए आप आए गए

जिसकी फुर्क़त से मोहसिन शिकायत न थी
उसके क़िस्से सभी को सुनाए गए

बैठे बैठे हम ये कैसे जाल में उलझ गए.
यार फिर से हम तिरे ख़याल में उलझ गए.

उनसे कैसे खद्दोखाल के तक़ाज़े पूरे हों.
छोड़ कर जबीं जो तेरे बाल में उलझ गए.

क्यों हमारे ही उलझने पर हो तन्ज़ जब के याँ.
अच्छे अच्छे हुस्न ओ जमाल में उलझ गए.

सिर्फ इक सवाले वस्ल था उसी पे हंस के बोले.
छोड़िए न आप किस सवाल में उलझ गए.

वो भी जा बसा कहीं किसी के साथ और फिर
मोहसिन भी घर की देख भाल में उलझ गए

Moni Chaudhary

Name=Moni chaudhary
email=monirocking287@gmail.com
Instagram id=@ink_slinger_28
              @the_creative_mvk
Already worked as co-author

बारिश में हुआ मेरा जन्म

बारिश का आना, मुझे ये बताना
देखो यह मौसम है सुहाना
मुझ बारिश से कुछ ना छुपाना।
छम-छम आती है ,मुझे ये बताती है
यह मौसम है तुम्हारा ...तुम्हें जीना है दुबारा।
रिम-झिम बरसती है
मुझसे ज्यादा मुझे समझती है
फिर मुझसे कहती है
ना भूलना यह दिन
यह जन्म तुम्हारा, यह कर्म तुम्हारा,
तुम्ही को लिखेगा
न कभी बिकेगा
न कभी मिटेगा।।

रात के रंग में ढल जाए

सारी दुनिया से बहार
आतें है दिन के पार
केवल रात होती है जिसका सार
जिस में मिलता है हर खूबसूरत ख्वाब
तारों के नाम।।

दिन में ना जाने कितने दुख किस-किस से है पाए,
फिर रात में खुशियों के तारे है छाए,
दिन से जोभी मुसीबतें है लाए,
वो रात होते- होते ,
रात के रंग में ढल जाए.....

Shubham Rane

Meet shubham rane, he is currently working as peramedic and he's residing from a beautiful state called Goa. Apart from writing loves to travel and dance. Being a writer, he is been part of many anthologies. He wanted to explore himself and to reach in every person's heart through his piece of writing.

It's Winter Here So...

Close the windows and shut the door,
Gather up your homies
and light up the fireplace tough.
Hello, it's winter here so..
Make some hot delicious food
On the dinner table,
put on the headphones and
Listen to the words of music
as they babble.
Hello it's winter here so..
Get on the bed
and pull up your blanket,
With the story book in hand
Turn On the heater and let it go.
Hello, it's winter here so...
While going out from home
Wear a warm clothes,
Clear the snow from your footpath
Then smash it by your shoes.
Hello, it's winter here so...

Govind Narayan Joshi

He is writer

एक छोटी सी ख्वाइश है जो टूट सी गई है,
पता नहीं पर लगता है कि वो रूठ सी गई है.....!

सोचता था कभी मौका मिले तो खुल कर बातें karunga,
ये लगता है अब की कभी भी खुल का नहीं कह sakunga...!

लगता था तुम्हारे साथ कुछ वक़्त बिता खुल के रो लूंगा,
पर अब सब कुछ खुशी से अकेले ही अपने में सेह लूंगा.....!

सभी अपने रूठ से गए है अब हमेशा के लिए,
क्या मैं तुम्हारी आंखों में हमेशा जिन्दा रहूंगा.......!

दिल तन्हा सा हो गया है अपनों के तलाश में,
क्या थोड़ा सा प्यार दे कर रख तो सकोगे ना......!

एक बात है

कहते है कि इंसान अजीब है,
पर अजीब तो उनके सवाल है...
कोई इंसान है जिसके अंदर इतना कुछ है,
पर वह कभी किसीको सही से कह नहीं पाता...
एक है अपना जो बहुत तड़प रहा है,
बस अपनेपन और प्यार के लिए.....
वह अपने दिल की baatien कह रहा है,
पर उसे पता ही नहीं है कि वह क्या कह रहा....
कोई अपने खामोशियों के भीतर
बहुत बड़ा तूफान समेट कर बैठा हुआ है....
पर सच है ज़िन्दगी बहुत गुलज़ार है
बस यही एक बात है.....!!!!!

Gaurav Dubey

Well I belong from Raipur, love to write and dance and most importantly I am like a smoke, barely seen too long in one place, I can only stay where there is fire in person who can hold on to my thoughts.

My day starts and ends with you,
My talks begins and finishes with you
There is still that I could not get till now,
Whats there between us thats holding me amd how,
Even when you are gone,
My heart tells me wait! Hold on!
She is not gone.
Yes, there is a promise I made and I will keep.
I will keep all my promises I made before I take the final
sleep.

Pramesh Kumar

Pramesh Kumar, a writer who writes from his innermost.He is a budding and blooming personality in literature and in the literary world. He alway tries his best to put his head and heart on paper by his pen. His minute observation of worldly things and aspects gives a charm in his writing. Whatever he writes he tries to give a personality to his poem which conveys his innermost to his reader.He rightly says about his writing, "Every word of my writing is not only a combination of letters but my heartbeat which gives life to my literary arts".

A Gentle Kiss Of Love

A gentle Love's kiss…It seems more than a bliss
And that Love is you….You know well what to do.
You kiss me to make me smile
Every moment I am eager for a while
The more sensations are growing
The more feelings they're showing.
A gentle Love's kiss….Is something , forever exists
You are the one whom I know
And you help me forever to shine and grow
Yes it is gentle Love's kiss
That is something I ever miss
One thing to express that I do
Yes I loved, I love and will love you !

Anjali Samundre

अपने दिल के जज़्बातों को पन्नो पर उतारकर रखती हूं, मै लेखिका हूँ जनाब! सादगी का रूप रखकर अपने लफ्ज़ो को सँवारकर रखती हूं। मैं अंजली समुंदरे, मै जबलपुर(म.प्र.)की रहने वाली हूँ।

तुम

दूर हो के भी इतने पास हो तुम
गैरों की इस दुनिया में में अपना से एहसास हो तुम
मेरी शाम की दुआ और सुबह की पहली सोच हो तुम
मेरी ज़िन्दगी की नई शुरूआत हो तुम
मेरी खुशियों की चाबी हो तुम
मेरी पहली और आखरी चाहत हो तुम...

दिल की बात

ये दिल की बात हैं कैसे बताऊ
 राज़ है इस दिल में कैसे छुपाऊ,
कई बातें हैं तुम्हें बताने के लिए पर अब तुम ही बताओ तुम्हे मै कैसे
सुनाऊ ये दिल की बात हैं कैसे बताऊ।
तुम रूठ जाते हो यू बातों-बातों में मेरे जाना!मै तेरी इस नाराज़गी को
कैसे मिटाऊ ,
तुम मेरे ही तो हो मैं तुम पर अपना हक़ क्यों न जताऊ
ये दिल की बात हैं कैसे बताऊ।।

Aisha Chhetri

I am Aisha Chhetri from Darjeeling pursuing my degree in English. Poetry is what I love the most because it is the only way in which I can express my feelings and emotions

Oh Dream

The bag which once used to carry my dreams
Has now became a product of material
Now my contemplate of future only shows a deep darkness,
Is this because of the remorse that has turned into
concomitant worries??
The remorse that leads me to that decision -
Ahh! The sane decision between passion and profession,The
simplest yet the hardest decision to take.
But I have stride on from that now
Where even its souvenir starts to crumble,
I swamped! Swamped in life
Will I be able to take off again??
Such question lingers in my head
Over and over again ….Yet unanswered...

Stain

I see a red stain in her pant
not the stain in reality
but the stain of impurity
tagged by the society
The sham impurity
doesn't allow her to walk
in a kitchen or in a temple
it's the stain of restrictions
The stain that caged her
once in every month
is actually a shit
this society has formed
Why Impure?....she questioned to them
Amphonic all of them, cause they know it's all pure!

दिव्यांशु पांडे "बिट्टू"

लेखक का नाम दिव्यांशु पांडे बिट्टू है। यह भारत में बलिया जिला के उत्तर प्रदेश के निवासी हैं। लिखना, पढ़ना और अच्छे लोगों से बात करना इनकी रूचि है ।यह नाट्य कला में भी रुचि रखते हैं एवं थिएटर से जुड़े हुए हैं। इसके साथ-साथ ये मेडिकल विभाग में भी आयुर्वेदिक डॉक्टर बनने की तैयारी कर रहे है।इनके पिता का नाम श्री नित्यानंद पांडे है । इनकी माता का नाम श्रीमती शारदा पांडे हैं। यह कई एंथॉलजी में Co-author के तौर पर काम भी कर चुके हैं।

"हाइकु विधा में कविता"

१.ठीक है बढ़ो,
एक विक्रेता बनो!
खमीर धरो ।

२.सुखद नहीं,
यह वक्रता करो!
जमीर धरो।

३.इनायत है,
बृहदकथा तुम्हारी!
समीर बढ़ो।

४.बेचना पर,
गुणों का भी!
पहले खरीद करो।

५.जीत होगा,
काम शबाब करो!
समीप चलो।

६.गरीब रहो,
पर अमीर दिल!
करीब रखो ।

उम्मीद है यह हाइकु-संग्रह आप सभी को पसंद आया होगा।

Prachi Sharma

She is Prachi Sharma. She live in Ghaziabad in U. P. She pursuing bsc maths. Her first anthology as a co author A HEART TRAPPED MILLION OF EMOTIONS. She also works as a compiler in two anthologies WRITE TO FEEL NOT TO EXPLAIN and WRITER'S WORLD. Give your feedback on email (prachisharma51689@gmail.com). Instagram id (@sharma0162).

Khuyaish

Khuyaish tara jism ki nhi
Khuyaish teri khubsurti ki nhi
Khuyaish tara dil churana ki nhi
Khuyaish tara dil   ma choti sa jaga ki ha
Khuyaish teri dukh ki nhi
Khuyaish teri har khushi ki waja bana ki ha
Khuyaish tujh kamiyab dekhni ki ha
Khuyaish teri roh sa judna ki ha
Khuyaish ki Tu har janam milna ki ha
Ya pyar yuhi rahay barkar humara
Kabhi tu asa pagal ho …
Kabhi ma asa pagal ho
Khuyaish tujh sath rahna ki ha
Ya iss janam ya uss janam.

Priyanka K. Tiwari

Priyanka had a poetic disposition from childhood on. Her first poem was published in a newspaper when she was 8. She has written many poems in English and Hindi, some of which appeared in local newspapers and magazines. A graduate in Biotechnology, she is currently associated with the field of HR- Organizational Psychology. Travelling, photography and reading are her passions. She can be reached at - Instagram: @pri_at_insta
and via email at words.verses.dreams@gmail.com

Hope

Hope is the soul of life
Hope is life's motivation
Follow your hopes with hope
And with the greatest dedication.
Let hopes grow within you
Into reality, let them bloom.
For even if they stay unreal
They still drive away gloom!

One Autumnal Morn*

The sky is clad in deep, damp shades,
Hanging mystically over the lonely glades.

Tints of scarlet, lime, mauve and gold,
The overwhelming mystiques of the woods unfold.

Mist lies low over the craggy vales,
Rugged and beaten by the autumnal gales.

The emerald-hued foliage, all dripping with pearly dew,
Drown the wooded landscape in a clear, transparent hue.

Blossoming luxuriantly the lilacs and daffodils
And daisies, carpet the distant rolling hills.

These still, serene woods in the hours small,
Abound in the sights and colours of the fall.

Raza Sahil

Lives in City Amravati
Business cotton business

सब यार हमको जो बदनाम कर रहे हैं
हम है कि उनका ही अहतराम कर रहे हैं
हम इश्क़ ओ मुहब्बत को आम कर रहे हैं
मज़हब सिखाता है जो वहीं काम कर रहे हैं।
हम को खरीद ले साहिल अब किसी भी सूरत,
बाज़ारे इश्क़ में खुद को बेदाम कर रहे हैं,
वो आ बसा है हम में या हम उसी में कैद है
क्यों ज़िक्र उसका ही सुबहो शाम कर रहे हैं,
मालूम है हक़ीक़त हमको ये जानते भी है
क्यों आप बात को अब इबहाम कर रहे हैं
कुछ काम तो यक़ीनन मुझ से निकल के आया है
यूँ ही नहीं जनाबे साहिल सलाम कर रहे हैं
आप को जो ज़िंदगी पर एतबार है बहुत
फिर मसअला तो आपका दुश्वार है बहुत
मय्यत पर पहोच तो जाएंगे वक़्त पर
मसरूफ आज कल जो मेरे यार है बहुत
ऐ शाहज़ादी इश्क़ नहीं कर सकूंगा मै
के मुझ गरीब पे घर का भार है बहुत
मंज़िल पे ही नज़र रखे चलते रहो सदा
ये मत देखो कि इस राह में खार है बहुत
तुम एक ही शख़्स से मिले हो जानेजा फकत
मुझ में छुपे हुए अभी किरदार है बहुत
तनहाइयों के खौफ से जो शख़्स मर गया
अब मिल्कियत में उसके भी हक़दार है बहुत
आसां है जंग जीतना लेकिन मै क्या करुँ
मेरे कबीले में ही जो गद्दार हैं बहुत
एक दिन भंवर के बीच में डुबोएगा रज़ा...
.जिस शख़्स पर भी आपको एतबार है बहुत.........

Vijay Thakur

Simple person.. Shaayar badnaam

ना जाने के यह वक़्त आगे बढ़ गया बहुत
या हम बहुत पीछे रह गए दुनिया से !!
वक़्त ही आगे चला गया होगा
 शायद बहुत हमसे!!
के उमीदों को अपनी अक्सर
चाह के भी पकड़ नहीं पाते हम !!
ये कहाँ आ गए हम........
खुद और आईने के बीच ही
कशमकश लगी रहती है हर दम के
अब तो तुझको भी ऐ ज़िन्दगी
कहा खुल के जी पाते हैं हम !!
ये कहाँ आ गए हम........

Meet Dixit

Meet Dixit belonging to Rajasthan has done his schooling from Banswara and at present he is working and exploring the environment. He's a professional guy by the day and a poet by the night. He did his MBA from Ahemdabad itself and is now looking for better prospects. He's looking forward to get lost in the world of writing and poetry. His perspective towards the world is different as he wants to get better person constantly with the moto of Go high by having feet on the ground.

Saccha Pyaar

Jab ruthe ho khudse to ek sath chahiye,
Jab ankhe ho nam to ek bar puchne wala chahiye,
Jab jatana ho pyar to koi ruthne wala chahiye,
Kuch naa bolu to bhi samjhe woh ek pyaar chahiye,
Mere ek tarfa pyar ko samjhne wala chahiye,
Shayad gussa hou usse to samjhane wala chahiye,
Mai jab khoya hu uski yado mai tab ek jhalak uski chahiye,
Jab jazbaato ko samjha na pau to woh sath chahiye,
Ankho ko nam dekh ek muskan ki chah chahiye,
Tiktok ke zamane mai woh khat wala pyaar chahiye,
Jab baate na ho paaye to mulakat chahiye,
Mohabbat ko shadi ka naam de aisa ab sath chahiye,
Jab toot jau mai khudse to hath thamne wala chahiye,
Night life ke dor mai suhani sham wala sath chahiye,
Jo gulab na de to sahi magar ab uska hath chahiye,
Shayad isliye ek sacche pyaar mai ek saccha dost chahiye.
Ab saccha pyar hi chahiye

Flairs and Glairs, a platform by a student for the students. We are esteemed youth struggling to carve out our path for our future and we follow a basic mindset Since everyone is not born with all-round skills. Joining hands with people who are born to execute it with perfection is the best way to evolve. Self-Evolution is the need of the hour but, evolving as a community is what we strive for. The initiative as kickstarted by, Founder- Mr. Shubham Shah with the motive to utilize the skillset and talent of writing has now a team of 10+ people who are actively participating into newer forms of learning and discovering talents among youngsters. We Provide platform and services like Publishing opportunities, Open mics, Workshops, Hands-on training. Operating with Brand Name of Flairs and Glairs (Publication House), we offer the chance of elevating a passionate writer to an esteemed author With Brand name Teekhe Zasbaaat. We bring to you an opportunity to get accustomed with the Public Speaking and Presenting of Thoughts along with regular challenges to brush up your inking spirit. The newest initiative to extend our services we introduced in a new writing Platform- The Glittering Fables and Ink Over Tears.

We Choose to Fly Like A Falcon than to be

a Leg Pulling Crab.

To Know More: Infoline – 7781900870
Mail Us At-
flairsandglairs@gmail.com / info@flairsandglairs.in
Or Visit is at
www.flairsandglairs.com / www.flairsandglairs.in
Social Handles- @flairsandglairs @teekhezasbaaat